P9-CQO-676

the BAD GUYS

in

INTERGALACTIC GAS

IF YOU PURCHASED THIS BOOK WITHOUT A COVER, YOU SHOULD BE AWARE THAT THIS BOOK IS STOLEN PROPERTY.
IT WAS REPORTED AS "UNSOLD AND DESTROYED" TO THE PUBLISHER, AND NEITHER THE AUTHOR NOR THE
PUBLISHER HAS RECEIVED ANY PAYMENT FOR THIS "STRIPPED BOOK."

TEXT AND ILLUSTRATIONS COPYRIGHT © 2017 BY AARON BLABEY

ALL RIGHTS RESERVED. PUBLISHED BY SCHOLASTIC INC., PUBLISHERS SINCE 1920. 557 BROADWAY,
NEW YORK, NY 10012. scholastic AND ASSOCIATED LOGOS ARE TRADEMARKS AND/OR REGISTERED TRADEMARKS
OF SCHOLASTIC INC. THIS EDITION PUBLISHED UNDER LICENSE FROM SCHOLASTIC AUSTRALIA PTY LIMITED.
FIRST PUBLISHED BY SCHOLASTIC AUSTRALIA PTY LIMITED IN 2017.

THE PUBLISHER DOES NOT HAVE ANY CONTROL OVER AND DOES NOT ASSUME ANY
RESPONSIBILITY FOR AUTHOR OR THIRD-PARTY WEBSITES OR THEIR CONTENT.

NO PART OF THIS PUBLICATION MAY BE REPRODUCED, STORED IN A RETRIEVAL SYSTEM, OR TRANSMITTED IN ANY
FORM OR BY ANY MEANS, ELECTRONIC, MECHANICAL, PHOTOCOPYING, RECORDING, OR OTHERWISE, WITHOUT WRITTEN
PERMISSION OF THE PUBLISHER. FOR INFORMATION REGARDING PERMISSION, WRITE TO SCHOLASTIC AUSTRALIA, AN
IMPRINT OF SCHOLASTIC AUSTRALIA PTY LIMITED, 345 PACIFIC HIGHWAY, LINDFIELD NSW 2070 AUSTRALIA.

THIS BOOK IS A WORK OF FICTION. NAMES, CHARACTERS, PLACES, AND INCIDENTS ARE EITHER THE PRODUCT OF
THE AUTHOR'S IMAGINATION OR ARE USED FICTITIOUSLY, AND ANY RESEMBLANCE TO ACTUAL PERSONS,
LIVING OR DEAD, BUSINESS ESTABLISHMENTS, EVENTS, OR LOCALES IS ENTIRELY COINCIDENTAL.

ISBN 978-1-338-18957-5

10 9 8 7 6 5 4 3 2   20 21 22 23

PRINTED IN DONGGUAN, CHINA   95
FIRST U.S. PRINTING 2018
THIS EDITION SECOND PRINTING, JUNE 2020

Are we rolling? OK.

This is **TIFFANY FLUFFIT**
for Channel 6 News.
Our television station has been
destroyed, but we will keep
broadcasting as long as we can.

This is what we know . . .

6 NEWS

Tiffany Fluffit
6 NEWS

1

Well, the flesh-eating zombie kittens were bad,

but they were **NOTHING** compared to this . . .

The world has been **OVERRUN** by zombie puppies,

zombie ponies, zombie dolphins, zombie bunnies,

and, yes—**MORE** zombie kittens!

We believe this to be the work of the **EVIL**

DR. RUPERT MARMALADE,

but he has **COMPLETELY**

DISAPPEARED!

MARMALADE

• CHAPTER 1 •
FLY ME TO THE MOON

I'm keeping our spirits up, *hermano*, with succulent pockets of meat and beans.

They're good, too. I've had **SIX** already.

How can you eat when the world is ending?

I eat for comfort! It makes me feel safe!

DON'T JUDGE ME!

Thanks, Piranha.

No sweat, *chico.*

As I told you when we first met, Mr. Snake,

the **INTERNATIONAL LEAGUE OF HEROES** is a secret organization.

The regular authorities don't know we exist. That's why we need to find another way to deal with this . . .

ggrghrjh!

What do you suggest?

We need to . . .
borrow a rocket and

GET TO THE MOON OURSELVES.

Borrow?

She means **STEAL.**

WHAT?! Oh noooo, no, no, **NO!**
That's NOT part of the plan. No one will EVER
believe we're **HEROES**
if we **STEAL** something.
Especially a rocket!
I mean, someone will
NOTICE if we **TAKE**
A WHOLE
SPACESHIP!

I won't
do it.

Mr. Wolf, listen very carefully.

The world IS about to end.

The **ONLY** way to stop it is to get

to the moon. And **WE** are the only

ones who know the truth.

If we don't . . .

borrow a spaceship and destroy

the Cute-Zilla Ray . . .

. . . . EVERYONE ON THE FACE OF THE EARTH WILL DIE.

PERIOD.

Well, if you put it like that . . .

But will we bring it back?

If we survive this mission and
SAVE THE EARTH,
I'm pretty sure they'll let us keep it.
But yes, we will try our hardest to
bring it back . . .

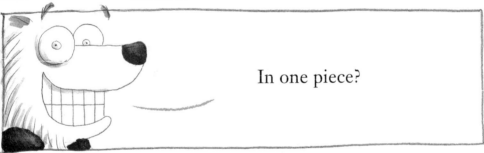

In one piece?

Um . . . sure.

OK, I guess that's cool.

So, we need to find a spaceship, come up with a plan to get inside it, and then you'll fly us to the moon?

Well, yes.
Except that last part.
I don't know how to operate a spacecraft . . .

WHAT?!

But if you can't fly a rocket, how is this stupid plan supposed to work?

I never said *I'd* be flying . . .

Then who will?!

· CHAPTER 2 ·
WE HAVE LIFT-OFF

Are you sure about this, Agent Fox?

. . . rocket?

Sir! We have orders to get this booster rocket onto that spaceship! The world's gone crazy, huh?

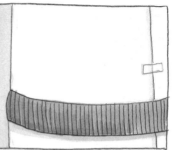

That's pretty small for a booster rocket . . .

Yes, it is. But this little beauty is **FULL** of surprises.

SECURI

As you were . . .

SECURITY

Wow. That was amazing! How did you *do* that?!

It's all about **CONFIDENCE,** Mr. Wolf. You just need to believe you can do it, and everyone else will believe it, too.

Yeah, yeah, I'd LOVE to hear more of this thrilling motivational speech, but can you PLEASE JUST GET US OUT OF HERE?!

OK. Let's do this.

Guys?
Go inside and get
in position . . .

Anyone want
a burrito?

You need
professional
help.

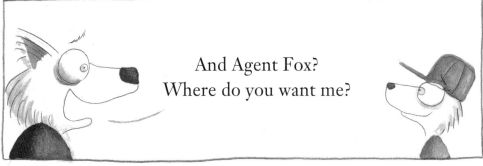

And Agent Fox?
Where do you want me?

That's not for me
to say, Mr. Wolf.
This is **YOUR** mission.

What?

Do you mean . . .
YOU'RE NOT
COMING?!

Someone has to
stay here and fight
the zombies . . .
and that means us—

FLING!

TWIRL!

THE INTERNATIONAL LEAGUE OF HEROES!

NO! We can't do this without you! We're not **HALF** the heroes you are!

You're more like us than you know!

In fact, we used to be **JUST LIKE YOU**.

Maybe I'll tell you about it some day.

But right now, you have to go and save the world.

WE'RE COUNTING ON YOU.

We won't be able to hold back the zombies for long . . .

Wolfie! Hurry! We have to get out of here **RIGHT NOW!**

Strap in, Wolfie! This will probably be a little rough . . .

OK! Get ready! In . . .

5! 4! 3!

2! 1!

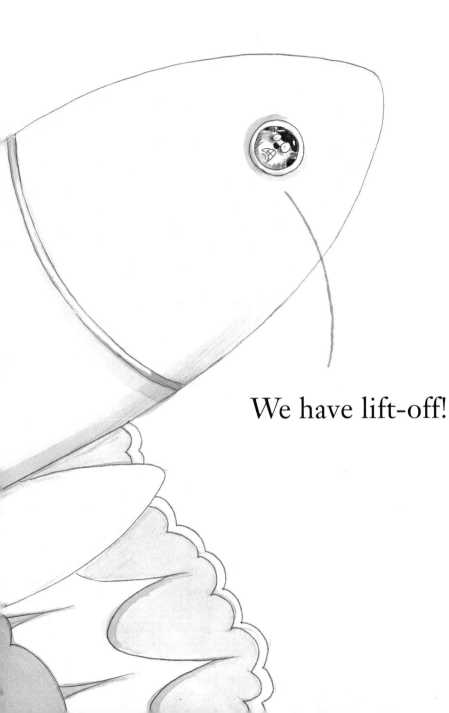

We have lift-off!

And
remember,
guys—
we bring
this rocket
back in
one piece!

Hang on, Wolfie. Just separating
the boosters . . .

• CHAPTER 3 •
ZERO GRAVITY, ZERO JEALOUSY?

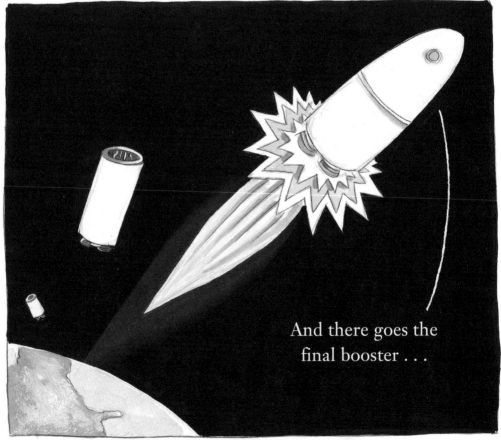

And there goes the
final booster . . .

Seriously?!

That's the last one, Wolfie. I promise. The *rest* of the ship will stay in one piece. But hey! Look!

ZERO GRAVITY!

Let's go for a float!

Oh man. I'm freaking out, guys. I feel terrible that we **STOLE** this rocket. **AND** we have the fate of the world in our hands. **AND** Agent Fox . . . well . . . she isn't here. I need a sign that we're doing the right thing! Please! **GIVE ME A SIGN . . .**

SPLAT!

Yo, *chico*!
My burrito bag burst.
Grab that, will you?

This is serious, Piranha!

How many of these have
you eaten, anyway?!

I'd rather
not say . . .

Don't give him a hard time just because you're scared, Wolf.

I'm sorry! I just didn't think being a hero would be quite this stressful . . .

WHATEVER!

YOU keep getting us into these situations, so **DEAL WITH IT!**
If we survive, your precious Agent Fox will give you a **KISS.**
And if we don't . . .
well, it won't matter, will it?

Just saying.

And Wolf?

Yeah?

You told us once that we needed to show the whole world that we're heroes.

You said we just needed to do something that would make the whole world **SIT UP AND NOTICE**.

Well, this is your chance.

Oh. Yeah.
Whatever.

This is it, boys!

I'm going down to put on a

SPACESUIT.

It's time to go be a . . .

CHAPTER 4

EVERY SNAKE FOR HIMSELF

OK, fellas. I'm bringing us in to land.

It looks quiet enough out there. But, Wolf? Are you still down in the **LOADING BAY?**

You really should get back up here. Landing might be a little bumpy . . .

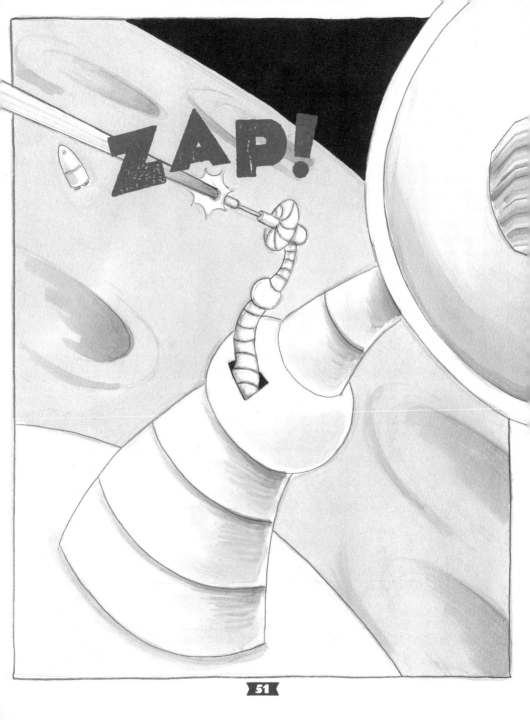

We're hit!

VOOOOOSH!

There's a hole in the ship!

WE NEED TO SEAL IT! WE NEED TO SEAL OFF THE COMMAND CAPSULE!

Snake! Wait!
Wolf's down there!
You'll trap him!

If we don't seal it . . .
**WE ALL
DIE!**

Snake! **NO!**

CLUNK!

Wolf!

VOOMP!

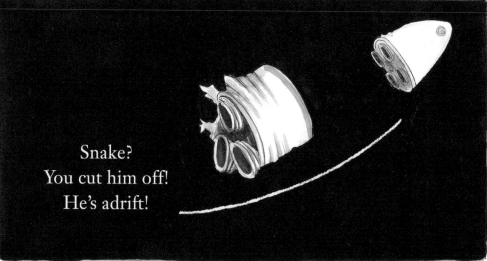

Snake?
You cut him off!
He's adrift!

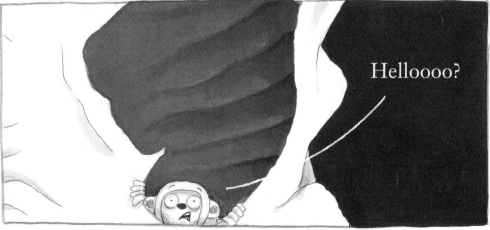

Helloooo?

On the bright side, at least I have a spacesuit . . .

WARNING!
OXYGEN LEVEL AT **15%**!
YOU WILL RUN OUT OF AIR IN 10 MINUTES!
OXYGEN LEVEL DROPPING!
OXYGEN LEVEL AT **14%**!
WARNING!

WARNING!
WARNING!
Hmmm . . .
okey dokey . . .

• CHAPTER 5 •
TIED UP . . . AGAIN

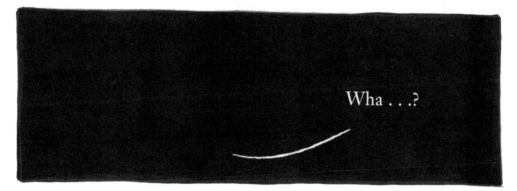

Wha . . .?

Where . . .
where am I?

Oh man.
This doesn't look good . . .

I don't get it. How
does Marmalade
ALWAYS manage to
knock us out and tie us
up? He's so small!

How've you been,
Mr. Shark? Eaten any
of your friends today?

That's none of your business,
you evil lunatic. The world is
ending because of **YOU!**

And . . . Mr. Wolf . . . you
saw what happened to our
lovely Mr. Wolf . . .

Leave me alone.

He's right, you little monster! Mr. Wolf **IS** your fault. You killed him! You shut that door before he had a chance . . .

YOU'RE LUCKY I CAN'T MOVE!

I can't believe you locked him out. Mr. Wolf **BELIEVED IN YOU!** And that's how you repaid him . . .

Wolf?!

Yes.

As you can see,
he's not quite dead.

He's alive? Wolf's alive!

Well, yes and no. You see, he's running out of air. And in precisely eight minutes, he'll stop being a hero . . . **PERMANENTLY**.

Bring him inside! Please, Dr. Marmalade! *Please!* Mr. Wolf is the best guy we know . . .

Oh. Well, if you put it like that, then . . .

...NO! I think it would be much more fun to watch him run out of air.

Especially since, you know, it's **ALL YOUR FAULT.**

You monster! If I wasn't tied down I'd—

You'd what?

You'd *cry* on me? Keep quiet, **LEGS**, or I'll pull off all your furry little digits and they'll have to start calling you **BODY** instead.

Hey . . . wait a minute . . .

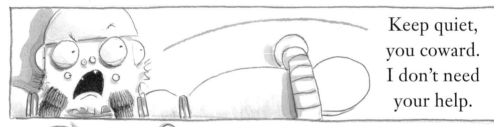

Keep quiet, you coward. I don't need your help.

No, no. Listen to me for a second . . .

Does anyone know
where Piranha is?

• CHAPTER 6 •

OH NO. ANYTHING BUT THAT . . .

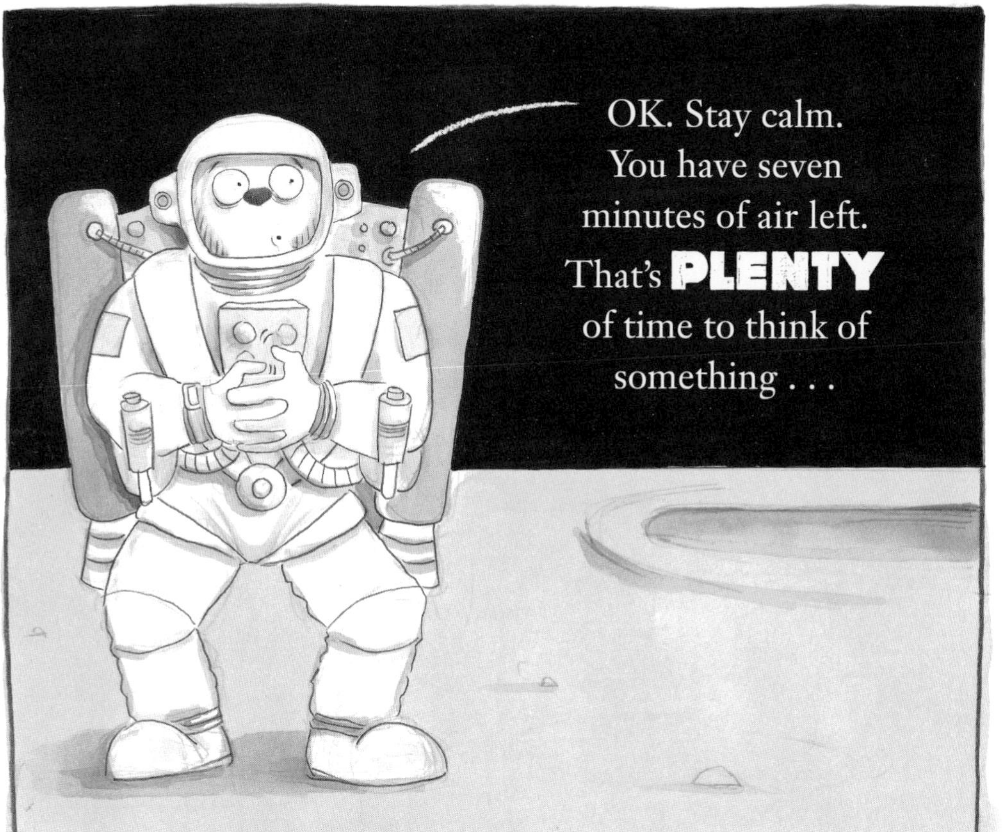

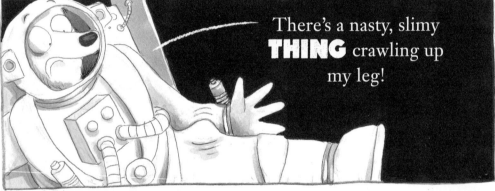

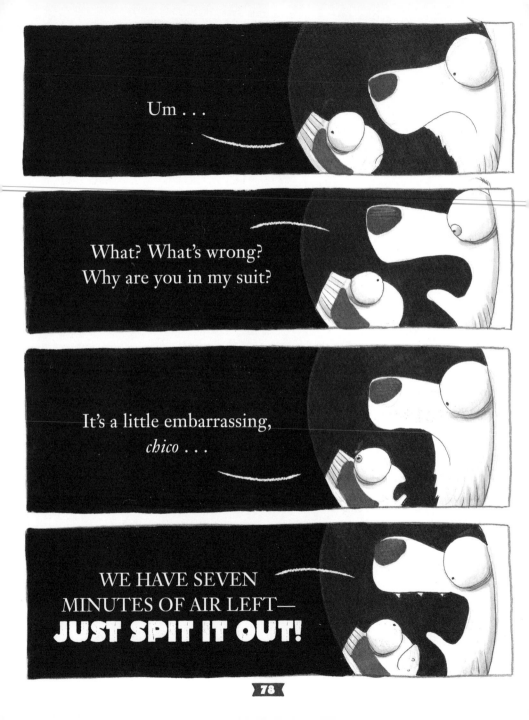

OK!

I ate too many burritos and I needed somewhere to poop!

I'm sorry, can you say that again?

I needed somewhere to poop out my burritos and **I DECIDED TO DO IT IN THE SPACESUIT.**

YOU POOPED IN THIS SPACESUIT?!
NO!
I was GOING TO but then you climbed into it! And then I just didn't know what to do next . . .
BUT WHY WERE YOU GOING TO POOP IN A SPACESUIT IN THE FIRST PLACE?!
IT'S A SPACESUIT!
WHO POOPS IN A SPACESUIT?!

YOU KNOW WHY WE'RE RUNNING OUT OF AIR? BECAUSE THERE'S A **POOP BURGLAR** IN HERE USING UP HALF OF IT. **THAT'S WHY!**

Wolf. Listen to me. If **ANYONE** can get us out of this mess, it's you.

But you need to *calm down*, *hermano*.

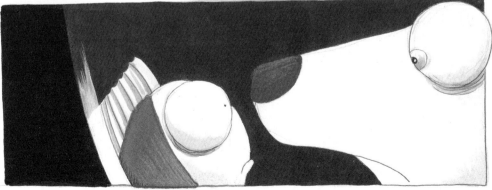

The situation can't get **ANY WORSE**, can it?

That's right! It can't! And you know what—

FAAART!

What was *that*?!

What was what?

FAART!

That! That sound!
And . . . and . . . that . . .
terrible **SMELL** . . .

PIRANHA, DID YOU JUST FART IN THE SPACE SUIT?!

Chico. I ate **SO MANY BURRITOS**. That's a **LOT** of beans, you know what I'm saying?

FFAARt!

· CHAPTER 7 ·
IN SPACE, NO ONE CAN HEAR YOU FART

Oh no!
Look at his face!
He's run out
of air! He can't
breathe!

Please, Dr. Marmalade! Please save him! Look! He's in **AGONY!**

That's weird.
He still has four
minutes of air left.

I wonder what
the problem is?

You know why?

No, I really don't . . .

Because I have a **JET PACK**. And **THAT** is a **BIG, SCARY DEATH-RAY THINGY**. And **YOU** are filling this suit with truly **POISONOUS GAS**.

What does that add up to, Mr. Piranha?

I have no idea . . .

Never mind.
You just keep farting and
I'll find a way to blow up
this machine . . .

No, wait! **I GET IT!**
You think the **FLAMES** from the
JET PACK and the **GAS** from my
FARTS will cause an
EXPLOSION that will destroy
the **CUTE-ZILLA RAY!**

That's right!

But . . .
There's no way we'll
survive that . . .

No one
said being
a hero was
going to be
easy, Mr.
Piranha.

· CHAPTER 8 ·
TIME TO BE A HERO

BACK ON EARTH . . .

Sure, it's cool to be in the **INTERNATIONAL LEAGUE OF HEROES**, but sometimes this job really sucks . . .

There are too many of them, Fox.
I told you **WE** should have taken
that spaceship instead . . .

Trust me.
Mr. Wolf will do it.
He'll destroy the
CUTE-ZILLA RAY.

Oh, isn't that sweet! He's going for one last joyride before the air runs out. Isn't he just adorable!?

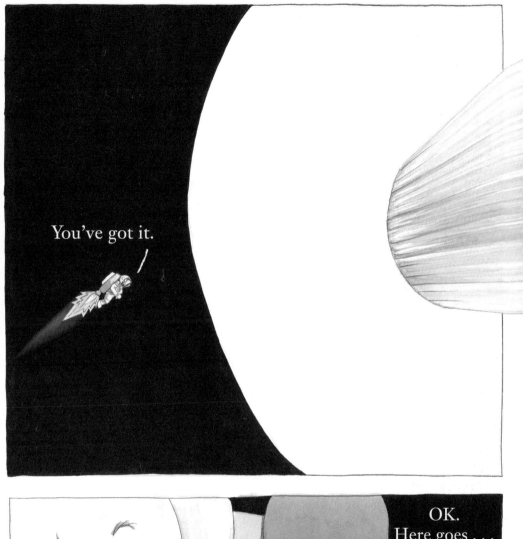

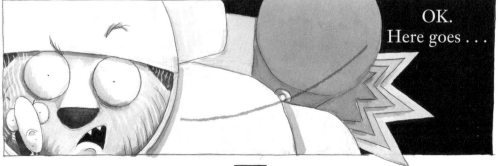

... NOTHING!

FIZZZZZ!

We're inside the
ray beam!

VOOMP!

Now let's get in there and

BLOW THIS THING TO BITS!

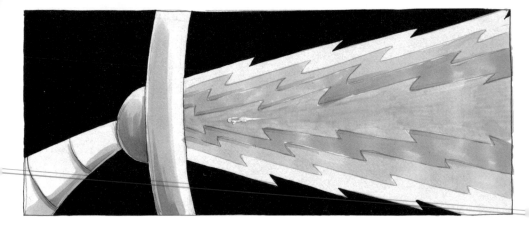

All right!
We're inside it!

I'll fly down
as deep as I
can and . . .

A **WINDOW!**

Just **FART** as much as you can. And I'll head toward those windows down there . . . Our plans have changed, Mr. Piranha . . .

Whatever you say, *chico* . . .

FAAART!

I think you mean

HELLO,

Dr. Marmalade!

Now, get a load of this—

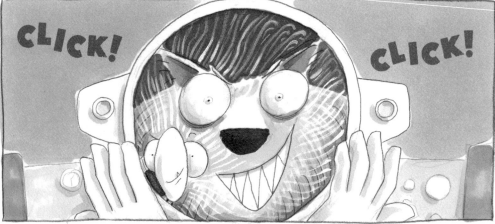

CLICK! CLICK!

Are we ready?

Wolfie, you're on!

Er . . . CITIZENS of THE WORLD!

My name is Mr. Wolf, and this is my team . . .

. . . the **GOOD GUYS CLUB!**

We really do need a better name, don't we?

First of all, I'd like to apologize for taking a rocket without permission. I feel really bad about that and—

Get on with it, man . . .

. . . OK . . . but mostly I want to tell you that **WE** have just put the evil Dr. Marmalade out of business up here on **THE MOON.** And it is my very great pleasure to give you back **PEACE ON EARTH!**

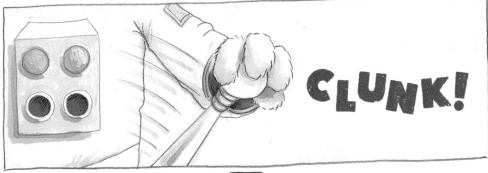

CLUNK!

Mr. Wolf!
You're officially
a HERO!

· CHAPTER 9 ·
WHEN IS A GUINEA PIG NOT A GUINEA PIG?

Wolfie!
They're partying
all over the world!

We saved
the world!

And everyone **KNOWS**
we saved the world!

Things might be a
little different now,
boys. Looks like we
might not be such
bad guys after all.

Snake?

Guess what? Shark's right—
I *was* jealous.

It made me happy when you
thought I could be a good guy,
Wolf. It really did.

But then that perfect Agent Fox
came along and . . . I just . . .
felt like a dirty old snake again.

I was mad at you.
And I . . .
I locked you out to save myself.

I know what I see.
And it's not just
a dirty old snake.
That's for sure.

HEY! Sorry to
interrupt your inexplicable
forgiveness of the snake,
but look who's waking up!

OH GOOD.

I know I'm a good guy
and everything, but this
is going to be fun . . .

No. He's grown **TWO TENTACLES** with **BUTTS** on the ends of them . . .

But that doesn't make any sense . . . guinea pigs don't have tentacles . . .

NO, THEY DON'T. BUT THEN AGAIN, I'M NOT REALLY A GUINEA PIG.

OK. Nobody panic.

But there's a *slight* chance that Dr. Marmalade might actually be an . . .

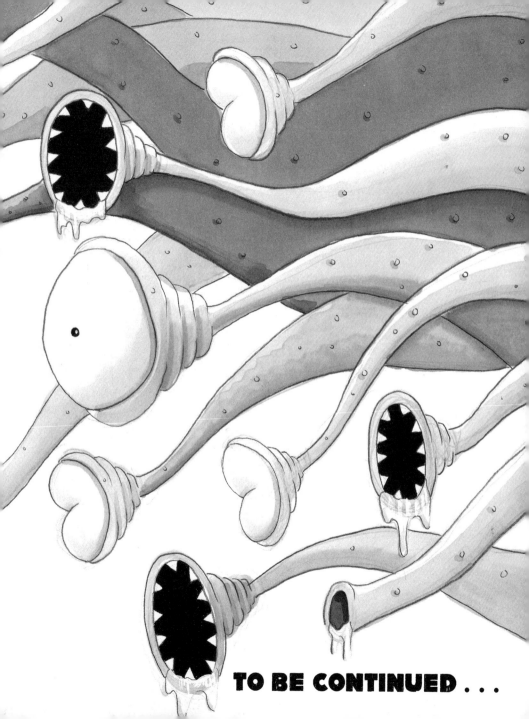

TO BE CONTINUED . . .

One by one, the **BAD GUYS** are vanishing.

TAKEN! By a creature with **WAY** too many teeth . . . and **FAR** too many bottoms.

Is this the end? Maybe. But will it be funny?

YOU BET YOUR BUTT IT WILL!

Don't miss *the* **BAD GUYS** *in Alien vs Bad Guys!*